# Little Bitty Friends

Elizabeth McPike · Patrice Barton

G. P. Putnam's Sons

G. P. Putnam's Sons
an imprint of Penguin Random House LLC
375 Hudson Street
New York, NY 10014

Library of Congress Cataloging-in-Publication Data
McPike, Elizabeth.
Little bitty friends / Elizabeth McPike ; illustrated by Patrice Barton.
pages cm
Summary: "Babies observe and make friends with friendly little animals"—Provided by publisher.
[1. Stories in rhyme. 2. Babies—Fiction. 3. Animals—Infancy—Fiction. 4. Friendship—Fiction.] I. Barton, Patrice, 1955- illustrator. II. Title.
PZ8.3.M46175Lit 2016   [E]—dc23   2014044993

Manufactured in China by RR Donnelley Asia Printing Solutions Ltd.
ISBN 978-0-399-17255-7
Special Markets ISBN 978-1-524-73873-0 Not for Resale
1  3  5  7  9  10  8  6  4  2

Design by Marikka Tamura.
Text set in Cooper OldStyle Demi.
The images were created using pencil sketches and mixed media
that were assembled and painted digitally.

This Imagination Library edition is published by Penguin Young Readers, a division
of Penguin Random House, exclusively for Dolly Parton's Imagination Library,
a not-for-profit program designed to inspire a love of reading and learning, sponsored
in part by The Dollywood Foundation. Penguin's trade editions of this work are
available wherever books are sold.

For my darling Kate, who saw and loved
the little things that only little eyes can see.

—E.McP.

For Brody, with love.

—P.B.

**L**ittle bitty steps,
marching one, two, three,

Little furry caterpillar,
tickle, tickle knee.

Little bitty buttercups,
reaching for the sky,

Little bitty bird,
learning how to fly.

Little bitty snail,
peeking from his house,

Little bitty nibble,
little bitty mouse.

Little weeping willow,
swaying in the breeze,

Little bitty nose,
little bitty sneeze.

Little bitty chipmunks,
chattering all the day,

Little bitty ladybug
always comes to play.

**Little bitty rest,
little blankie snug,**

A little pick-me-up . . .
and a giant, giant hug!